THE JUNIOR NOVEL

ADAPTED BY
SUSAN KORMAN

HarperCollins *Children's Books*

Kung Fu Panda™ & © 2008 DreamWorks Animation L.L.C.

First published in the UK by HarperCollins Children's Books in 2008

1 3 5 7 9 10 8 6 4 2
ISBN-10: 0-00-726926-9
ISBN-13: 978-0-00-726926-6
A CIP catalogue record for this title is available from the British Library.
www.harpercollinschildrensbooks.co.uk
Book design by John Sazaklis

Printed and bound in China

ONE

THUD! BANG!

Po the panda was in the middle of a familiar dream when he rolled over on his big round belly, fell out of bed, and crashed to the floor.

His eyes flew open. "Ouch . . . ," he murmured, rubbing his side. "That hurt!"

Po had been dreaming that he was a famous kung fu warrior, fighting dangerous assassins and protecting his village from harm. It was his favorite dream.

He tried to use one of those kung fu moves to kick himself to his feet, but his belly got in the way and he rolled back, still flat on his back.

"Po!" cried his father from downstairs. "What are you doing up there?"

"Nothing, Dad!" Po answered. He climbed to his feet, immediately jumping into another kung fu stance.

"Monkey! Mantis! Crane!" he said, calling out the names of the Furious Five, the most famous kung fu masters in all of China. "Tigress! Viper!"

"Po!" his father shouted one more time. "Let's go! You'll be late for work!"

"Okay!" Po called back. Still pretending to be a kung fu master, he grabbed a ninja star from the floor and threw it at the wall with furious might. But instead of piercing the wall with brute force, the star bounced right off. He chucked another star even harder . . . and the same thing happened. His prowess in his dream was not carrying through to his real life.

Finally, Po headed downstairs, struggling to fit through the narrow steps that led to the kitchen of his family's noodle shop.

"Morning," Po greeted his father. The panda didn't really look like his dad. For one thing, Po didn't have feathers, and for another, his dad was a goose!

"Let's go!" his father scolded. "The cabbage needs to be chopped; the carrots need to be peeled; and table three is waiting for their order—Secret Ingredient Soup."

"Sorry, Dad," Po mumbled.

Po's father sighed. "'Sorry' doesn't make the noodles, son," he said. "What were you doing up there, anyway? There was so much noise."

"Oh, nothing," Po answered. "I was having this crazy dream . . ."

"You were?" His father looked up from the vegetables he was chopping. "What were you dreaming about?" he asked.

"What was I dreaming about?" Po echoed.

"Uh . . ." He stalled, not wanting to tell his father the truth. "Uh, I was dreaming about noodles," he blurted out finally. "That's it, noodles!"

"Noodles?" Po's father repeated skeptically. "You were really dreaming about noodles, son?"

"Uh, yeah," Po answered, trying to sound casual. "What else would I be dreaming about?" He handed a noodle bowl to a customer.

"Oh, happy day!" Po's father exclaimed. "My son is finally having the noodle dream!" He threw an arm around Po, slipping an apron onto him. "You don't know how long I have been waiting for this moment. It's a sign!"

"Whoa, Dad," Po said uneasily. "A sign of what?"

His father beamed. "A sign that you are almost ready to be entrusted with the secret ingredient of my Secret Ingredient Soup! And then you will fulfill your destiny and take over the restaurant, just as I took it over from my father, who took it over from his father, who won it from a friend in a game of mahjong."

Here we go again, Po thought.

"It was just one dream, Dad," he cautioned his father.

"No, it was *the* dream," Po's father said excitedly. "We are noodle folk, Po. Broth runs through our veins!"

"But, Dad," Po started to ask. "Didn't you ever want to . . . I don't know . . ." He tried to find the right way to ask the question that was on his mind. "Didn't you ever want to do something else with your life? Do something besides make noodles?"

"Po, we all have our place in this world," his father answered firmly. "Mine is here, and yours—"

"I know," Po finished the thought for him, "is here, too."

"Actually," Po's dad said, "it's at table three. They're still waiting for their soup!"

And with that, Po's father handed him the order.

"Excuse me. Pardon me," Po murmured, as he tried to maneuver his large body across the restaurant, which was much too small and crowded to fit a giant panda. "A thousand pardons . . ."

two

The Jade Palace sat on top of a majestic mountain, high above the village that was nestled in the Valley of Peace. Outside the palace, a kung fu master named Shifu was playing a flute. Lost in the music, the small red panda didn't appear to notice the five dark shapes lurking in the bushes nearby.

Suddenly, the five figures burst from the shrubs and dived toward the kung fu master.

Shifu moved like lightning, deftly using his flute to deflect and block his attackers' moves.

One by one, the kung fu master sent the five figures flying through the air.

"Barely adequate!" he snapped at his five famous students. "Tigress, you need more ferocity! As for you, Monkey, you need greater speed!"

Each of them bowed respectfully to the master as he continued correcting their kung fu technique.

"Crane, you need height!" Shifu informed him. "And you, Viper, more subtlety."

Just then a palace goose ran up.

"Master Shifu!" the goose cried.

"What?" Shifu said impatiently.

"It's Master Oogway. He wants to see you," the goose said.

Shifu whirled around, rushing into the palace.

Inside the Scroll Room, smoke from candles and incense filled the air. Off to the sides, tall pillars with intricate carvings reached up to the ceiling.

The old tortoise waited near a reflecting pool in the center of the room.

"You wanted to see me, master?" Shifu asked nervously, his long, white whiskers twitching. "Is something wrong?"

Master Oogway stared at him. "Why must something be wrong for me to want to see my old friend?" he asked.

"So . . ." Shifu still wasn't convinced. "Nothing's wrong?"

"Well." The wise old tortoise hesitated for a second. "I didn't say that."

Shifu waited.

Oogway opened his mouth but didn't speak. To Shifu's surprise, he blew out a candle, and then another, and another.

Impatient, Shifu stepped over and spun his ringed tail around. In a swift kung fu move, he extinguished all the candles at once.

Then he turned back to the tortoise. "You were saying, master?"

Oogway nodded. "I have had a vision," he

began. "And my vision is that Tai Lung will return."

"*Tai Lung?*" Shifu gasped. "Oh no!" His eyes automatically flitted around the room, where a terrible battle had taken place long ago. The walls were still scarred with angry claw marks.

"That is impossible," Shifu said. "Tai Lung is in prison, master."

"For now," Oogway replied.

A palace goose stood nearby.

Shifu whirled around and grabbed him. "Zeng!" he commanded. "Fly to Chorh-Gom Prison at once. Tell them to double the guards, double their weapons. Double everything! Tai Lung does not leave that prison!"

"Yes, sir! Yes!" the goose answered. "Of course!" He flew off.

"It will not matter, Shifu," Oogway said quietly. "One often meets his destiny on the road he takes to avoid it."

"But we have to do something, master," Shifu urged him. "We can't just let Tai Lung march on the Valley of Peace and take his revenge. He'll—He'll—" Shifu sputtered, afraid to think about exactly what Tai Lung would do if he did indeed return to the valley.

Oogway slowly approached the Water of the Moon reflecting pool. He used his staff to stir the water. "Your mind is like this water, my friend. When it is agitated, it becomes difficult to see. But if you allow it to settle, the answer becomes clear."

Shifu nodded, trying to quiet his thoughts and push aside the frightening images of Tai Lung.

Together they stared into the water. As it settled, an image from the ceiling was reflected back at them: an intricately carved dragon, clutching a scroll in his mouth.

"The Dragon Scroll," Shifu whispered.

Oogway nodded. "It is time," he said.

Back at his father's crowded noodle shop, Po was busy serving customers.

Just then a palace goose rushed into the shop and slapped a poster onto the wall.

Po went over to read the announcement from the Jade Palace.

"Master Oogway's choosing the Dragon Warrior! Today!" he called out.

Customers stared blankly at him.

"Everyone!" Po cried. "Go! Get to the Jade Palace!"

The restaurant patrons all rushed to finish their food.

"This is the greatest day in kung fu history!" Po exclaimed. He started to run for the door.

"Po!" his father called. "Where are you going?"

Po hesitated. "To the Jade Palace."

"But you're forgetting your cart," his father said.

"My what?" Po asked.

His father gestured to a noodle cart. "The whole valley will be there," his father said eagerly. "And you can sell noodles to all of them.

I told you that your dream was a sign!"

"Sell noodles?" Po echoed in dismay. "But, Dad, you know, I was kind of thinking that maybe I could . . ." His voice trailed off as he took in the excited expression on his father's face. Then he let out a sigh. "I was thinking that maybe I could also sell the bean buns," Po said finally.

"That's my boy!" Po's father declared in delight. "Excellent idea!"

Po went over to get the noodle cart, trying to hide his disappointment. While everyone else in the valley watched Master Shifu choose the Dragon Warrior, he would be stuck working, selling noodles to the crowd.

three

Later that afternoon hundreds of villagers streamed into the large Jade Palace theater.

Po stood with his noodle cart at the bottom of the towering steps that led up to the palace.

"Come on, baby," he told himself. "Let's do this."

He was out of shape, but he could make the climb; he knew he could.

Slowly, he started up the steps, lugging the noodle cart behind him.

The hot sun beat down on him. "Come on," he said. "Come on. We're almost there."

He stopped for a second, flopping onto his back to catch his breath. Looking down, he realized he had made it up only seven steps so far.

"Oh no!" he moaned. At this rate he was never going to make it to the top to see the action.

Two pigs hurried past.

"Sorry, Po," one said, chuckling at Po's plight. "We'll bring you a souvenir, okay?"

"Yeah," the other one snorted. "Catch you later!"

"No!" Po declared, his eyes narrowing as he watched them dash up the steps. "*I'll* bring me back a souvenir."

With a burst of energy, Po yanked off his apron and hat and tossed them onto the ground. Then he went back to climbing up the long set of steps.

Meanwhile, inside the theater, Master Oogway reached the bottom of the palace stairs, where Shifu waited for him.

A palace pig banged a gong.

"Are your students ready?" Oogway asked Shifu.

"They are," Shifu said with a nod.

"Now know this, old friend," Oogway said. "Whomever I choose will not only bring peace to the valley. The Dragon Warrior will also bring peace to you."

Shifu bowed at the wise tortoise, and then together they approached the roaring crowd that had gathered in the theater.

A palace pig banged a gong to announce their arrival. "Let the tournament begin!" he called.

Meanwhile, Po had finally made it to the top step.

"Yes!" he congratulated himself, panting hard. "I did it!"

Then, right in front of his eyes, the doors of the theater slammed shut.

"No!" Po cried. "No, no! Wait!" He ran over to the doors and banged hard. "Please! Open the door! Let me in!"

Drums pounding inside the arena drowned out the sound of Po's knocking.

Spectators roared as Shifu stepped to the center of the ring.

"Citizens of the Valley of Peace!" he said dramatically. "For one thousand years, we have waited for the Dragon Warrior of legend, the one who will bring peace to our valley. But now the wait is over."

Oh no, Po thought desperately. *I'm missing everything!* He spotted an open window and hurried over. Still panting from his long climb up the steps, he pulled himself up and peered inside.

Shifu was about to introduce his star students. "It is my great honor," he said, "to present to you . . . Tigress! Viper! Crane! Monkey! Mantis!"

One by one, the Furious Five jumped into the center of the ring.

"Today, one of these five kung fu champions will be chosen as the Dragon Warrior!" Shifu announced.

"Wow!" Po drew in a breath. There they were—his idols—the most amazing kung fu stars in the Valley of Peace.

Just then a strong gust of wind knocked Po down and blew the window shut.

Inside, the Furious Five readied themselves.

"Warriors, prepare!" Shifu called out.

Po glanced around desperately. Finally, he spotted a peephole in the door. "Oh, good!" he cried. "A peeky hole!"

"Master Crane! Ready for battle!" Shifu announced.

Po watched through the crack as Crane spread his wings. "Wow," he murmured. "The Thousand Tongues of Fire!"

Suddenly, a spectator inside the arena stood in front of Po, blocking his view.

"Whoa!" murmured the pig, as Crane soared toward the sky. "Look at that!"

"Hey!" Po cried frantically. "Get out of my way!"

He backed up, trying to get a better look at Crane—and toppled down the steps.

Inside the theater, the crowd gasped in awe at Crane's acrobatic show. "Incredible!"

"That was amazing!" someone cried. "I've never seen anything like it!"

One by one, the Furious Five performed.

Po desperately tried to get inside. He found a pole and attempted to vault over the side of the theater. Instead, he landed flat on his back. Next, he rigged a catapult out of a tree, but that didn't work either.

"Believe me, citizens, you haven't seen anything

yet!" Shifu announced from inside the ring.

"That's for sure," Po murmured. Suddenly, he spotted a rope tied to a tree.

"I know!" he declared, getting an idea.

"Master Tigress!" Shifu blared. "Face Iron Ox and his Blades of Death!"

While Tigress set up her move, Po used the rope to swing himself high in the air. He got a quick peek at the powerful-looking tiger before landing hard in a fireworks cart.

After the Furious Five had finished demonstrating their expert moves, Master Oogway stepped into the center of the arena. He raised his hand, and the crowd instantly hushed.

"I sense the Dragon Warrior is among us," Oogway said solemnly.

Shifu motioned for the Furious Five to gather in the center of the ring. "Citizens of the Valley of Peace," he called out. "Master Oogway will now choose . . . the Dragon Warrior!"

Shifu looked at Oogway and bowed. Oogway

nodded and closed his eyes. Inside the theater it was completely still.

At long last they would all learn the name of the mighty Dragon Warrior.

four

P o could hear Shifu's announcement from where he lay inside the fireworks cart. "Oh no!" he cried. "They're choosing the Dragon Warrior! I'm missing it!" He glanced around frantically. All around the cart were powerful explosives. "Yes," he murmured. "That'll do it."

Working fast, Po tied a load of fireworks to a chair. Then he hopped on and lit the fuse.

Po's father had been looking everywhere for him. "Po!" he cried, finally spotting him. Then he saw the fireworks tied to Po's chair. "What are you doing, son?" He rushed over and tried to blow out the fuse.

"What does it look like I'm doing?" Po shot back. "Stop! Stop, Dad! I'm going to see the Dragon Warrior!"

"But . . ." Po's dad stared at him. "I don't understand, son. What about the noodle dream? You finally had the noodle dream."

Po watched the fuse, burning closer and closer to the fireworks. "I lied, Dad," he blurted out. "I don't really dream about noodles. I love kung fu!"

Po closed his eyes and gripped the chair, getting ready for takeoff. But a second later he was still on the ground.

"Oh no," he said. The fuse was a dud.

Po's father held out Po's apron. "Come on, son. Let's get back to work."

"Okay," Po agreed sheepishly. His father was right. He should be selling noodles, not spending his time on kung fu.

With a sigh, Po reached for the apron.

BOOM!

The fuse had suddenly lit the fireworks tied to the chair. Po blasted upward over the arena, sending a shower of fireworks into the air.

"Come back!" Po's father yelled.

The crowd below watched the explosion of color. *"Oooooh!"* they cried in awe. *"Aaaahhhh!"*

Po soared up, up, and up . . . until finally the fireworks died out.

"Uh-oh," Po whispered, knowing what was coming next.

Below him, Oogway raised his hand. He was ready to name the Dragon Warrior.

SMASH!

Before Oogway could say anything, Po landed in the center of the ring with a big crash. A huge cloud of dust and smoke engulfed the giant panda.

Slowly, Po opened his eyes. To his astonishment, he was facing Oogway . . . who was pointing a long claw at him.

Po looked around in confusion. "Okay . . ."
He fumbled to explain. "I just wanted to see
who the Dragon Warrior was. And now, I'm,
uh, going. . . . Sorry to disturb you all."

A strange smile flickered across Oogway's
face. "How interesting," he murmured.

Po tried to duck out of the way, but
Oogway's claw followed him wherever the
panda moved.

Tigress stood behind Po. "Master," she asked
in confusion. "Are you pointing at me?"

"No." Oogway shook his head. "I'm pointing
at him," he replied.

"Who?" Po said.

Oh boy, he thought, an odd sensation
rippling through him. For some reason the old
tortoise was pointing straight at Po.

five

"I'm pointing at you, panda," Oogway said softly.

"Me?" Po echoed.

Then, before he could say or do anything more, Oogway lifted Po's paw with his staff and held it up for everyone to see.

"The universe has brought us the Dragon Warrior!" Oogway announced triumphantly.

"What?" Po said.

"What?" the Furious Five said in unison.

"What?" cried Shifu.

"What?" Po's dad shouted.

Just then a palace pig banged the gong loudly—the signal that the Dragon Warrior had been chosen.

The crowd cheered wildly as Po stood there, utterly bewildered. Confetti rained down everywhere.

Me? I'm the Dragon Warrior? he thought. *This can't be happening.*

He felt himself being hoisted into the air, and then placed onto a palanquin—a seat carried on poles. Straining under Po's tremendous weight, the palace geese carried him out of the theater.

Meanwhile, Shifu was horrified by the scene unfolding before his eyes.

The panda is the Dragon Warrior? he thought. *This can't be!*

Shifu elbowed his way through the crowd, desperate to reach Oogway.

Finally, he caught up with him.

"Master Oogway! Master Oogway!" Shifu

panted. "Wait! That flabby panda cannot possibly be the answer to . . . to . . . our problem!" he blurted out. "Please, you were about to point at Tigress!" he went on. "That thing fell in front of her. It was an accident!"

Oogway smiled gently. "There are no accidents," he told Shifu.

Suddenly, there was a loud *thud*!

Shifu looked over. Po was so heavy, he had burst through the bottom of the palanquin. A squad of burly pigs immediately rushed over. They hefted Po onto their shoulders, along with the palanquin and the geese who'd been struggling to carry the giant panda.

Shifu watched in dismay as they continued on their way to the Jade Palace.

The Furious Five were in shock, too.

"Forgive us, master," Tigress said to Shifu, bowing her head. "We have failed you."

"No," Shifu replied grimly. "If the panda is still here by morning, then *I* will have failed *you*."

six

I t was dark when Zeng, the palace goose dispatched by Shifu, finally reached his destination.

In the moonlight, Chorh-Gom Prison was an ominous sight. The huge jail was carved into the side of a frozen mountain. Made of iron and rock, it towered over the landscape, fifteen stories high. It had no windows, and only one door, which was bolted and sealed tight. Several rhinoceros guards clad in armor patrolled the grounds.

As soon as Zeng landed, the guards pointed their spears at him.

"Wait!" the goose cried. "Wait, wait, wait! I bring a message for your commander." He held up the scroll from the palace.

The rhinos kept their spears pointed.

"It's from Master Shifu!" Zeng added urgently. "It's very important!"

Within minutes, the terrified goose stood in front of the commander—a furious-looking rhino covered in armor. He even had a metal plate covering his horn.

"What?" the commander bellowed as he read the scroll. "Shifu is telling me to 'double the guards'? I need to take extra precautions because my prison may not be 'adequate'?"

The guards held their spears near the goose's throat as he quaked in fear.

The commander snapped the scroll shut. "You doubt my prison's security?" he roared, scowling at the goose.

"Absolutely not!" Zeng reassured him.

"Well, Shifu does, sir." He laughed nervously. "I'm just the messenger."

"I'll give you a message for your Master Shifu!" the commander growled. "Escape from Chorh-Gom Prison is impossible!

"Come! I will show you!" He turned and walked away.

The rhino guards led Zeng through underground corridors until they reached an enormous cavern. A small bridge stretched across a deep canyon.

"Whoa," the goose murmured, looking out over the precipice into the vast cavern.

The commander clapped the goose on the back, sending a feather drifting down below. "Impressive, isn't it?" he said.

"Very, very impressive!" the goose honked. "It's very impressive!"

"One way in, one way out," the commander bragged. "We have one thousand guards and just one prisoner."

"Yes, sir, except . . ." Zeng gulped. "That one

prisoner is Tai Lung," he finished nervously.

"Come with me!" the commander ordered. "You will see for yourself. There is no way to escape from Chorh-Gom Prison!"

The commander led the way to an elevator. It wasn't much of an elevator: a wooden platform hung suspended over the canyon by one long metal chain. Several rhino guards pulled on ropes to winch them down, the platform swinging from side to side. As they descended, the commander deliberately shook the elevator, trying to frighten the goose.

It was working.

"What are you, crazy?" Zeng demanded. "Stop it!"

The commander just laughed. The elevator finally plunked onto a rock ledge, sending an echo throughout the prison.

Next, they passed through a series of locked doors, one after another. Then a drawbridge was lowered in front of them. It led onto an island that rose up from the canyon floor.

"Oh my," Zeng murmured. "This certainly does seem secure."

Abruptly, the commander halted. "Behold, Tai Lung!" he announced.

Ahead, a large, shadowy figure crouched on a rock.

The goose glanced at him and then turned around. "I'll, um, I'll just wait right here, okay?" he said.

The commander laughed. "There's nothing to worry about, goose! It's perfectly safe."

With that, he shoved Zeng in front of him.

"Ooof!" The goose stumbled forward.

"Crossbows at the ready!" the commander ordered the rhino guards.

Slowly, the goose stepped toward Tai Lung. The giant snow leopard, who had once been a powerful, majestic-looking cat, now barely showed signs of life. His large body was trapped inside armor made of tortoiseshell, and each of his front paws was chained to a heavy boulder that hung off the side of the thin island. As the goose and the commander stepped closer, Tai Lung didn't even look up.

"Hey, tough guy," the commander taunted him. "Did you hear? Oogway is finally going to give someone the Dragon Scroll, and guess what, buddy—it's not going to be you!"

The goose stared at the commander in disbelief. "What are you doing?" he said. "Don't get him mad!"

"What's he going to do about it?" the commander scoffed. "I've got him completely immobilized!"

The commander stomped on Tai Lung's tail.

"Ouch!" Zeng murmured, flinching. But the snow leopard didn't react at all.

"Aaaawwww." The commander wasn't finished taunting Tai Lung. "Did I step on the wittle kitty's tail?" he said, pretending to sound sympathetic. "Poor kitty . . ."

Tai Lung still didn't move. Instead, his eyes stared ahead coldly, showing absolutely no sign of life or emotion.

The commander turned back to the goose with a smug expression. "Do you see now? It is not possible for Tai Lung to escape," he said.

The goose nodded, relieved. "I've seen enough. I'll tell Shifu he's got nothing to worry about."

"That's right," the commander repeated. "There is nothing to worry about."

"I'm sorry for ever doubting you," Zeng added quickly.

"You don't need to apologize to me," the commander snapped. "Apologize to my guards." He gestured to the army of rhino guards above them. "All one thousand of them."

Zeng swallowed hard and turned to the guard standing closest to him. "I'm—I'm—sorry if I offended you," he blurted out. "And you, with the crossbow," he added. "Sorry, too!"

Satisfied, the group turned away from Tai Lung, who lay still near their feet, his eyes half closed. As they started toward the drawbridge, none of them noticed the goose feather that had drifted down in front of Tai Lung. With one swift, slick move, the snow leopard reached out with his tail and snatched it.

SEVEN

"**D**ragon Warrior! Dragon Warrior!"
The crowd chanted loudly as the
group of burly pigs carried Po into
the Jade Palace with the palanquin.

Po looked up in wonder at the bright red
columns and jade green tile roof of the palace.
It was so amazing. Po couldn't believe he was
about to go inside!

The pigs deposited him in the hallway, and
then closed the doors, leaving him alone in the
Sacred Hall of Heroes.

Po suddenly felt a little nervous. *They can't really believe that I'm the Dragon Warrior,* he thought.

He ran over to the locked doors. "Wait a second!" he called. "Uh, I think there's been some kind of mistake here!" He knocked on the doors a few more times, but no one came.

Finally, he gave up and turned around. All around the room were dozens of kung fu artifacts, things that had been used by warriors from the past.

"Whoa," Po murmured in awe. "Would you look at this place? That's Master Flying Rhino's armor, with authentic battle damage! And the Sword of the Iron Warrior, said to be so sharp, you can cut yourself just by looking at it." He gasped. "There's the Invincible Trident of Destiny!"

Po ran all around the room, amazed by the ancient kung fu artifacts. Then something else caught his eye. He rushed over to look at an object sitting on a pedestal. It was the Urn of

Whispering Warriors.

"It's said to contain the souls of the entire Tenshu army," Po remembered. He stuck his head into the vase. "Helloooo?" he called. "Anybody in there?"

"Have you finished sightseeing?" a voice asked suddenly.

Po gasped in surprise. The urn was talking back! "Sorry," he said. "I should have come over to see you first."

Another reply came back instantly.

"My patience is wearing thin."

"Oh well," Po told the talking vase. "It's not like you're going anywhere."

"Would you turn around?" the voice snapped.

"Sure." Po spun around—and saw someone standing behind him, scowling. It was Master Shifu, who crossed his arms in annoyance.

"Hey, how's it going?" Po said. Then he turned back to the vase. "Now how do you get five thousand souls—"

Abruptly, Po spun around again. "Master Shifu!" he cried. His massive body lurched backward, knocking into the urn. It smashed to the floor.

"Oh no!" Po said. "Someone broke that. But I'm going to fix it. Do you have some glue?" he asked Shifu sheepishly.

Shifu glared at the clumsy panda standing before him. "So you're the legendary Dragon Warrior, hmmm?" he said sarcastically.

"I guess so," Po answered nervously.

Shifu smiled tightly. "Wrong!" he told Po, shaking his head. "You are not the Dragon Warrior. You will never be the Dragon Warrior until you have learned the secret of the Dragon Scroll!"

The teacher pointed to an elaborately carved dragon on the ceiling. In its mouth it clutched a single scroll.

"Cool," Po said, staring in awe. "The Dragon Scroll!" He turned back to Shifu. "So how does this work? Do you have a ladder or trampoline or something so I can get up there?"

Shifu glared at him. "You think it's that easy? That I am just going to hand you the secret to limitless power?"

"No, I . . ." Nervous, Po let his words trail off.

"One must first master the highest level of kung fu," Shifu snapped. "And that is clearly impossible if that one is someone like you."

"Someone like me?" Po echoed uncertainly.

"Yes!" Shifu declared. Slowly, he walked around Po, looking closely at him and poking various body parts with his staff. "You'll never master kung fu with this fat butt or these flabby arms," he scoffed.

Then he eyed Po's stomach. "And that ridiculous belly," he added, smacking him there.

"Hey!" Po protested.

Shifu sniffed him. "Not to mention, your utter disregard for personal hygiene."

"Now wait a minute!" Po argued. "That's a little uncalled for!"

"Don't stand that close to me," Shifu ordered. "I can smell your bad breath!"

"Listen." Po tried to tell him. "Oogway said that I was the—"

Shifu grabbed one of Po's outstretched fingers and pinched it hard.

Po grimaced. "Not the Wuxi Finger Hold!" he said.

Shifu grinned slyly. "Oh, you know this hold?"

Po nodded. "It was developed by Master Wuxi in the Third Dynasty."

"Oh, then you must also know what happens when I flex my pinkie," Shifu went on.

Po nervously eyed his finger, which was locked in Shifu's tight grip. He nodded quickly. "I know what happens," he muttered.

"You know what the hardest part of this move is?" Shifu asked. "Cleaning up afterward."

"Okay! Okay!" Po begged. "Take it easy. Please take it easy!"

"Now listen closely, panda." Shifu snarled at him. "Oogway may have picked you, but when I'm through with you, I promise, you're going to wish he hadn't. Are we clear?"

Po nodded vigorously. "Yes, yes. We're clear. We are *soooo* clear!"

"Good." Shifu let go of Po's finger, finally satisfied. "I can't wait to get started!" he said in a tone that made Po nervous—very, very nervous.

eight

Po was still nursing his wounded finger a little later, when the doors to the training hall slid open. Inside were all kinds of equipment for working out, including a harrowing obstacle course full of spinning spikes and moving wooden clubs. The Furious Five were also there, training and performing some of the most dazzling kung fu moves that Po had ever seen.

His jaw dropped as Tigress pulverized a swinging, spiked ball made of wood, sending splinters everywhere.

"Let's begin here," Shifu said, gesturing to the gauntlet.

Po's eyes went wide. "Wait, wait, wait! Now?"

"Yes, now!" Shifu snapped back. "Unless you think the great Oogway was wrong, and you are not the Dragon Warrior!"

"Oh, well, I—I—" Po stammered. "I don't know if I can do all of those moves."

"Well, if we don't try, we'll never know, will we?" Shifu said smugly.

"Uh, yeah," Po tried to explain. "It's just— maybe we can find something more suited to my level."

"And what level is that?" demanded Shifu.

"Well, you know," Po said. "I'm not a master yet. Let's just start at zero, level zero," he suggested.

"There is no such thing as level zero," Shifu retorted.

"Hey!" Po spotted a training dummy. It had a friendly looking smile on its face. "Maybe we can start with that!"

"That thing?" Shifu scoffed. "We use that for training children! And for propping open the door when it's hot," he added. "But if you insist . . ."

"I do!" Po said. As he turned toward the dummy, the Furious Five gathered around him to watch the training session.

"Wow!" Po exclaimed in amazement. "Here I am with the famous Furious Five." He looked at them more closely. "You're so much bigger than your action figures! Except for you, Mantis," he added. "You're about the same."

Mantis gave him a dark look.

"Go ahead, panda," Shifu said impatiently. "Show us what you can do."

"Um . . ." Po glanced self-consciously at the Furious Five again. "Are they going to watch?" he asked uneasily. "Or should I just wait until they get back to work?"

"Hit it!" Shifu commanded. "Hit the dummy, panda!"

"I mean, I just ate," Po said, stalling. "So I'm still digesting. You know what that means—my kung fu may not be as good as usual."

"Just hit it!" Shifu repeated.

Po took a deep breath. "All right," he murmured. He danced around the dummy, pretending it was a bad guy and trying to tune out the fact that six kung fu experts were watching his every move.

"Whatcha got, buddy?" he said in the dummy's face. "You got nothing because I've got it right here. You picking on my friends? Get ready to feel the thunder! I'm coming at you with the crazy feet. My feet are a blur. I'm a blur," Po went on as he danced in place. "You've never seen panda bear style; you've only seen praying mantis!"

"Would you hit it?!" Shifu demanded.

"All right, all right," Po replied.

He hit the dummy lightly, and it rocked back into place.

"Good," Shifu told him. "Why don't you try again? A little harder this time."

Po punched the dummy again, this time knocking it all the way backward. He turned back to Shifu, a proud look on this face. "How's that—" he started to ask.

WHAP!

Just then, the dummy swung back and smacked Po hard. Dazed, Po tripped and stumbled his way through the obstacle course.

The Furious Five watched the scene, half amused and half disgusted. They had never seen a demonstration like the one being put on by this enormous, bumbling panda.

A spiky tethered ball slammed into Po, sending him flying into the jade turtle exercise bowl that rattled him around.

"This will be easier than I thought," Shifu

remarked to the Furious Five. "The panda will be gone in no time."

"I'm feeling a little nauseous," Po called out suddenly.

The jade turtle exercise bowl spilled him out, and he stumbled into an army of spinning wooden clubs that were studded with metal points.

"Ow! Those are hard! Oooh! I think I . . . *Ooof!*" The last club slammed into him hard.

"Ooohhhh!" Po gasped. He reached out to grab a pole, so he could pull himself to his feet.

That was a mistake. Immediately, it spun him around, and Po got pummeled all over again.

When Po emerged out the other side, battered and bruised, he found himself standing on a floor covered with small tubes that shot out bursts of flames.

"Yikes!" Po cried, feeling his feet get singed. He hopped across, trying to blow out the flames.

Finally, he managed to crawl over to a safe part of the room. He looked up at Shifu, who'd been watching Po's "workout" with a look of astonishment on his face.

"So," Po wanted to know, "how did I do?"

Shifu stared at him for a full minute before answering. "Thanks to you, panda, there is now a kung fu level zero!"

nine

After the workout session, the Furious Five walked back to the bunkhouse, which was perched on a hill near the training hall. None of them could believe what they'd seen today.

"We've waited a thousand years for the ultimate kung fu warrior," Tigress moaned. "One would think Master Oogway would choose someone who actually knew kung fu."

"Or one who could even touch his toes," Viper put in.

"Or even *see* his toes," Monkey added with a sneer.

As Po trailed along after them, he overheard every word they were saying about him. By the time they reached the bunkhouse, he hung back, too embarrassed to follow them inside. Instead, he waited outside by himself until they went to bed.

At last, the lights in the bunkhouse went out.

"Whew." Po breathed a sigh of relief and then crept up the bunkhouse steps. Unfortunately, as the heavy panda tiptoed through the hallway, the floorboards creaked loudly.

"Sshhh!" Po whispered. Tentatively, he took a few more steps forward.

Cre-e-aaak! Chunk!

This time Po's foot crashed through the floor. As he tried to recover, he made more loud noises.

Squeak-squeak-squeak-THUNK!

Po stumbled forward, banging through a bedroom door and landing on his back.

When he opened his eyes, he saw Crane staring down at him.

"Oh, hey," Po fumbled. "You're up!"

"Am now!" Crane replied dryly.

"I was just . . . uh . . . Woo! Some day, huh?" Po blurted out.

Crane stared at him, not saying a word.

"Whew!" Po blundered on. "That kung fu stuff is hard work! Are your biceps sore?"

Crane glanced at his wing. "I've had a long and rather disappointing day," he answered. "So I should probably get to sleep right now."

"Yes, of course," Po said.

"Okay, thank you," Crane replied.

Po started to leave, but he couldn't help turning back toward Crane to say one more thing. "It's just . . . aw, man. I'm such a big fan of yours," he confessed.

Crane smiled politely.

"You guys were totally awesome at the Battle of Weeping River," Po went on. "You were outnumbered one thousand to one, but you didn't stop, man, you just . . . Hi-YAH!" Po performed a series of clumsy-looking kung fu moves—and kicked a hole right through the paper wall.

From the other side of the wall, Monkey peered through the hole that Po had just made. He scowled at Po.

"Oh! Sorry about that," Po mumbled.

Crane wasn't too happy with him either. "Look, you don't belong here," he told the panda.

Po hung his head. "I know, I know. I'm not sure why Oogway picked me either. I'm just a big, fat panda. My whole life, I've been nothing but a—"

"No," Crane interrupted. "I meant, you don't belong here, as in this room. It's my room. Property of Crane."

"Oh, okay. Right," Po said, flustered. "I get it. You want to go to sleep."

"Yes." Crane nodded. "Exactly."

"And I'm keeping you up," Po went on.

"When we've got lots to do tomorrow. All right. The last thing I'm going to say is, you're awesome. Good night now."

Finally, he left the room, shutting the door behind him.

Crane let out a deep sigh of relief.

Po popped right back into the room. "What was that?" he asked.

"I didn't say anything," Crane replied.

"Oh. Okay," Po answered. "All right then. Good night. Sleep well."

Out in the hallway, he scolded himself. "I'm so stupid. I can't believe I did that."

Sighing, he searched along the corridor for an empty bedroom where he could sleep. The floorboards groaned again under his heavy footsteps.

Suddenly, Tigress opened one of the doors and stuck out her head.

Po winced when he saw the angry look on her face. "Oh, hey, Tigress," he said, putting on a chirpy voice.

"You don't belong here, panda," she snapped.

"Sorry," Po apologized. "I'm, uh, just trying to find an empty room. I'll keep trying."

"You don't belong in the Jade Palace," Tigress went on. "You're a disgrace to kung fu, and if you have any respect for who we are and what we do, you will be gone by morning."

Po looked around nervously. The rest of the Furious Five stood in their doorways, glowering at him. When Tigress was finished, they all slammed shut their doors, leaving Po standing there all alone.

ten

You're such a loser, Po told himself dejectedly as he went back outside. He sat under a peach tree in the moonlight. *You're not the Dragon Warrior—or any kind of warrior! You can't even do kung fu!*

"I see you have found the Sacred Peach Tree of Heavenly Wisdom," a familiar voice called out.

Po spun around, his face dripping with peach juice. Oogway stood nearby, looking at him with a curious expression.

"Is that what this tree is?" Po mumbled, his mouth stuffed with peaches. "I am so sorry, Oogway. I thought this was just a regular peach tree."

Oogway nodded. "I understand," he said. "You eat when you are upset."

"Upset?" Po shook his head. "I'm not upset. Why should I be upset?"

"So why are you upset?" Oogway asked.

Po sighed. It was no use trying to lie to wise Master Oogway.

"I stunk today," Po blurted out. "I probably stunk more than anyone else ever stunk in the history of kung fu, in the history of China."

"You're probably right," Oogway agreed.

"And the Furious Five totally hates me," Po went on.

"Totally," Oogway echoed.

"How's Shifu ever going to turn *me* into the Dragon Warrior?" Po asked. "I mean, I'm not like the Furious Five. I've got no claws, no wings, no venom. Even Mantis has those . . ."

He imitated the insect's front legs. "Thingies in front." Po sighed. "Maybe I should just quit now and go back to making noodles."

"There is a saying," Oogway replied. "Yesterday is history, tomorrow is a mystery, but today is a gift. That is why it is called the present."

At that, Oogway reached out and rapped the tree with his staff. A peach fell from the tree, landing right in Po's open paw.

eleven

I nside his cell in Chorh-Gom Prison, the snow leopard Tai Lung clutched the feather left behind by the palace goose. Holding it in his tail, he quickly used it to pick the lock that trapped him inside the heavy tortoiseshell armor.

By now the commander and palace goose had reached the main gate. Zeng was still trying to apologize to the stern commander. "I'm sorry. I apologize if we—"

Just then an alarm blared, cutting him off.

The commander looked around, startled. "I told the guards never to ring that bell," he said, "unless the prisoner . . ."

They raced over to the ledge to peer into the canyon below.

They saw that Tai Lung had thrown off the armor that had shackled him. He was now struggling with the heavy chains.

"He's loose!" Zeng yelled in a panic. "He's trying to escape!"

The commander barked out orders. "Fire crossbows!"

Instantly, the rhino guards fired spears at Tai Lung. The clever snow leopard dodged them and used the sharp spears to break open the cuffs around his wrists. He was free of the chains!

"Tai Lung is free!" the goose cried. "Tai Lung is free! I must warn Shifu at once!"

The commander slapped a hand over Zeng's mouth. "You're not going anywhere, goose!" he growled. "And neither is Tai Lung." He turned to the guards. "Bring up the elevator!" he ordered.

"He's coming this way!" Zeng shouted.

"He won't get far," the commander said. "Archers!" he yelled to the guards. A squadron of rhinos with bows and arrows fired at Tai Lung, who used the arrows to create a stairway on the side of the wall.

The agile snow leopard reached the elevator and hung from the bottom as more arrows rained down around him. The wooden platform was covered with a spiky blanket of arrows, but Tai Lung was unharmed.

The guards retaliated by cutting the chain, and the elevator crashed back down to the bottom of the pit.

Tai Lung swung up from the bottom of the elevator platform, catching the guards by surprise. He grabbed the chain and jumped onto a narrow ledge.

Minutes later he was on the bridge, racing toward the commander and the rest of the army.

"We're dead," the goose murmured. "So very, very dead."

"Hush!" the commander shushed him. "Not yet we're not. Now!" he ordered his men.

Archers set off explosives along the ceiling, sending massive stalactites crashing down onto the bridge. It began to crumble.

With a powerful leap, Tai Lung launched himself into the air and jumped from falling boulder to falling boulder, slowly climbing upward. Eventually he reached the top and grabbed hold of the final string of explosives and slung it down at the guards.

Zeng turned to the commander. "Can we run now?" he wanted to know.

"Yes!" the commander replied. "Run for your life!"

KA-THOM!

A second later, the door to the prison blasted open. As the prison exploded, rhinos flew everywhere.

The goose crashed to the ground. Groggily, he tried to sit up.

Suddenly, he felt paws close around his throat.

"I'm glad Shifu sent you," Tai Lung growled. "I was beginning to think I'd been forgotten." He smoothed the goose's ruffled feathers almost tenderly. "Fly back to Jade Palace, goose," he added in a low voice. "And tell them this: The Dragon Warrior is coming home!"

With that, he tossed the goose into the air. Terrified, the goose fluttered off toward the Valley of Peace.

Above him, white-hot lightning lit up the black sky.

twelve

Early the next morning, a gong sounded outside the Jade Palace bunkhouse. The Furious Five quickly gathered at the entrance to the training hall.

Shifu stepped up to them. "Where is the panda?" he demanded.

Tigress shrugged. "His room is empty," she said.

"And he wasn't at breakfast," Monkey put in.

"Mmmm," Shifu said, looking pleased. "I will give Master Oogway the unfortunate news."

"I'm afraid we were a little hard on him last night," Viper admitted.

"Do not blame yourselves," Shifu said smugly. "If the panda were the true Dragon Warrior, he would not have quit."

As they entered the training hall courtyard, Shifu let out a startled gasp.

Po straddled two sawhorses, his legs spread wide apart in an awkward-looking split.

"What are you doing here?" Shifu demanded.

"Morning, Master!" Po replied. "I thought I'd warm up a little."

Shifu eyed Po more closely. "You're stuck in that position, aren't you?" he asked.

"Stuck?" Po echoed, giving a little laugh. "Yes," he admitted a second later. "I'm stuck. I can't move."

Shifu looked at Crane. "Help him, please," he said.

Crane approached Po. "Oh dear," he murmured. Gingerly, he grabbed the panda's waistband and attempted to hoist him to his feet.

The huge panda didn't budge.

Embarrassed, Po flushed. "If you could just . . . Maybe on three, we can do it together. One, two, three . . ."

With Crane's help, he managed to get to his feet. "Oh, man," he said, relieved. "Thank you."

"Don't mention it," Crane murmured.

"No, really, I—" Po went on. "I appreci—"

"Ever!" Crane cut him off. "Don't ever mention it again." He walked away.

Shifu looked at Po. "You actually thought you could learn to do a full split in one night?" He laughed harshly. "It takes years to develop one's flexibility and even more years to apply it in combat."

He flung two boards into the air. Instantly, Tigress leaped up and executed a perfect split kick. As she landed, the broken chunks of board rained down near Po, knocking him in the head.

Still, he was in awe. "That was amazing!" he exclaimed, grabbing a piece of the board as a souvenir.

Then Shifu stepped forward. "Let's get started. There is only one way to learn how to fight, and that is to fight."

Viper squared up with Po. "Are you ready?" she asked.

"I was born ready," Po replied, trying to sound braver than he felt.

Viper swiftly lashed her tail around Po's wrist and wrenched his arm back. Po flew into the air and came crashing back down on his head.

"Sorry, brother!" she called out. "I thought you said you were ready!"

To everyone's surprise, Po sat up, grinning widely. "That was awesome!" he declared. "Let's do it again!"

The Furious Five looked at one another and then back at Po. For the first time, they couldn't help feeling a little respect for the panda.

He's clumsy, they thought, *but pretty tough.*

One by one, Po sparred with the Furious Five, each time falling flat on his face.

Finally, Shifu approached Po. "I've been taking it easy on you, panda, but no more," he said. "Your next opponent will be me."

The Furious Five exchanged uneasy looks.

"Step forth!" Shifu commanded.

Po had barely approached when Shifu whirled him around and threw him to the floor. Then he pinned Po's arm behind him.

"The true path to victory is to find your opponent's weakness and make him suffer for it," said Shifu.

"Oh, yeah!" Po said, smiling again.

Shifu whipped him around again, this time putting him into a finger hold.

"To take his strength and use it against him," Shifu went on. He held Po by the lip. "Until he finally falls—or quits!"

Shifu's words inspired Po. "But a real warrior never quits," he replied. "Don't worry, master. I will never quit!"

Frustrated, Shifu flung Po into the air and then leaped at him with a flying kick. The next thing Po knew, he was crashing out of the gates and skidding down the front steps.

The Furious Five watched him go.

"If he's smart, he won't come back up those steps," Tigress murmured.

"But he will," piped up Monkey.

Outside, they could still hear the panda groaning as he banged against each step.

"Ooh! Ugh! Ow! Ouch!"

thirteen

That night, after all the training—and bruising—he'd done, Po was sore.

Mantis was trying to relieve the panda's pain with acupuncture.

"*Aooo . . . Whoohoo . . . Eeeee . . . ,*" Po said, grimacing as Mantis inserted another needle through his skin. "I thought you said acupuncture would make me feel *better*, Mantis."

"Sorry," Mantis said, holding up a handful of needles. "It's not easy finding nerve points under all your—"

"Fat?" Po finished for him.

"Fur," Mantis said. "I was going to say fur. Honest."

"Sure you were," Po said skeptically.

"Who am I to judge a warrior based on his size?" Mantis went on. "I mean, look at me!"

"So what is Master Shifu's problem?" Po asked as Mantis inserted another acupuncture needle. "I know he's trying to inspire me, but if I didn't know any better, I'd say he's trying to get rid of me." He chuckled, and Mantis exchanged a look with Viper.

"I know he can seem kind of heartless," Mantis said. "But he wasn't always like that."

"According to legend," Viper chimed in, "there once was a time when Shifu actually used to smile."

"No." Po shook his head. He couldn't picture that at all.

"Yes," Viper replied. "But that was before . . ." Her words trailed off.

"Before what?" Po asked curiously.

Tigress had been listening from outside the door. "Before Tai Lung," she said, stepping into the room.

"Um, hey." Crane cleared his throat. "We're not really supposed to talk about that," he reminded her.

"Well, if he's going to stay," Tigress shot back, "he should know."

"What's to know?" Po asked. "I mean, I've heard the story: Tai Lung was a student, he turned bad, and now he's in jail. What's to know?" he repeated.

Tigress leaned in toward Po, making him nervous. "Tai Lung wasn't just a student," she said slowly. "Shifu found him when he was a cub. And he raised him as his son. It wasn't long before the boy showed talent in kung fu.. So Shifu trained him."

Po listened carefully as Tigress went on.

"Shifu believed in Tai Lung," she said. "He told him he was destined for greatness. But it was never enough for Tai Lung."

"What do you mean?" Po asked.

"He wanted the Dragon Scroll," she explained. "He wanted to know the secret to limitless power. But it wasn't meant to be. Tai Lung was driven mad by desire. He tried to take the scroll by force, not caring what, or whom, he destroyed. Shifu knew he had to stop him.

"But how could he?" Tigress added softly. She closed her eyes, remembering the story of how Shifu had tried to deliver a kick to Tai Lung, to prevent him from stealing the scroll.

"When Shifu saw the wounded look on Tai Lung's face," she went on, "he couldn't help himself. He stopped short. That was a mistake. Tai Lung instantly countered with a devastating strike and broke Shifu's leg."

"Yikes," Po remarked. "That must have been some strike."

"It was," Tigress replied. "Luckily, Oogway was there, too. When Tai Lung reached for the Dragon Scroll again, Oogway stopped him with strikes at his pressure points.

"Shifu loved Tai Lung like he'd never loved anyone before," Tigress continued. "Or since," she added, thinking about how often Shifu had corrected her when she was younger. In his eyes, she would never match the talent shown by Tai Lung.

A silence fell over the room.

"And now he has a chance to make things right, to train the *true* Dragon Warrior," she added bitterly. "But he's stuck with you—a big, dumb panda who treats the whole thing like a joke."

Just then, Po made a goofy face. *"Doiiiieeee,"* he said.

Tigress had had enough of his silliness. "That's it, panda!" she snapped. "Stop acting like a fool!"

"Wait, Tigress!" Mantis popped out from behind Po. "It's my fault," he explained quickly. "The panda is not making the face on purpose. I tweaked his facial nerve with a needle!"

At that moment, Po fell face first to the floor, his back still filled with acupuncture needles.

"And maybe I have also stopped his heart," Mantis murmured.

fourteen

Shifu sat inside the training hall, his eyes closed while he tried to meditate.

"Inner peace," he murmured. "Inner peace."

Finally, he opened one eye. "That's enough!" he snapped. "Would whoever is making that flapping sound please quiet down!"

Shifu resumed his meditation position.

The room went silent.

BOOM! Suddenly, Zeng dropped in from the ceiling.

"Ah, Zeng," Shifu greeted the goose. "Excellent. I could use some good news right now."

The palace goose blinked at him. "Uh, actually, Shifu . . . ," he fumbled.

Oogway was outside under the sacred peach tree, deep in thought when Shifu raced toward him.

"Master! Master!" Shifu cried.

"Hmmmm?" Oogway said, looking up.

Mist swirled all around them.

"I have . . . ," Shifu panted, out of breath. "It's . . . it's very bad news," he said.

"Ah, Shifu," Oogway said calmly. "There is just news. There is no good or bad."

"Master, your vision," Shifu went on. "Your vision was right. Tai Lung has broken out of prison. He's on his way!"

"That is bad news," Oogway remarked. He turned to face Shifu, an eyebrow raised. "*If you* do not believe the Dragon Warrior is capable of stopping him," he added calmly.

"The panda?" Shifu scoffed. "Master, that panda is not the Dragon Warrior! He wasn't even meant to be here—it was an accident!"

Oogway shook his head slightly. "There are no accidents," he reminded Shifu.

"Yes, I know," Shifu answered impatiently. "You've said that already. Twice."

"Well, my words were no accident either," Oogway said.

"That's three times," Shifu stated in frustration. This was a serious situation. Why wasn't Oogway getting it?

"My old friend," Oogway went on, "the panda will never fulfill his destiny, nor you yours, until you let go of the illusion of control."

"Illusion?" Shifu echoed. What in the world was Oogway talking about? This was a crisis!

"Yes, Shifu." Oogway tried to explain. "Look at this tree. I cannot make it blossom when it suits me, nor make it bear fruit before its time."

"But there are things we can control," Shifu insisted. "I can control when the fruit will fall," he pointed out, kicking the tree and making a peach drop at their feet.

Shifu tossed the peach into the air and then leaped up to split it with a chop of his hand.

He punched the ground, digging a small hole in the earth. "And I can control where to plant the seed," he added, placing the peach pit inside. "That is no illusion, Master Oogway."

"Ah, yes," Oogway said. "But no matter what you do, that seed will grow to be a peach tree. You may wish for an apple or an orange. But you will still get a peach."

"A peach cannot defeat Tai Lung," Shifu argued.

"Maybe it can," Oogway countered, "if you are willing to guide it and nurture it. And believe in it."

Oogway took a clump of dirt and covered the seed.

"But how?" Shifu asked. "How can I do that? I need your help, master," he pleaded.

"No," Oogway said emphatically. "You just need to believe. Promise me, Shifu. Promise me that you will believe."

"I . . . I . . ." Shifu hung his head. "I'll try," he said finally.

Oogway smiled, and then glanced up at the sky.

"My time has come," he said, looking back at Shifu. "You must continue your journey without me."

He handed his staff to Shifu.

"What?" Shifu was confused. "What are you talking about, master? I—"

Oogway backed away into the swirling fog.

"Master!" Shifu cried. "You can't leave me!"

Peach petals magically swirled around Oogway as he approached the edge of the cliff.

"You must believe," he called to Shifu. "You must believe!"

"Master!" Shifu cried again. "Please don't go!"

Desperately, he ran after Oogway. But it was too late. By the time Shifu reached the cliff, Oogway had disappeared into the swirling cloud of petals. There was nothing left but mist.

fifteen

"It's . . . delicious!" Mantis announced.

Po smiled modestly. He sat with the Furious Five at a table in the kitchen. He had just served them soup—the noodle soup that his father made at their restaurant.

"If you love my Secret Ingredient Soup, then you'd really love my dad's," he told them. "Dad actually knows the secret ingredient! That soup is delicious."

"Tigress, you've got to try this!" Monkey urged her.

She sat at the other end of the table, poking at a bowl of bland-looking white rice and tofu. "It is said that the Dragon Warrior can survive for months at a time on nothing but the dew of a single gingko leaf and the energy of the universe," she commented, giving Po a meaningful look.

He thought about this, his stomach rumbling. "I guess my body doesn't know it's the Dragon Warrior yet."

"Po," Mantis began, "you're really good at something. Why aren't you doing that instead of trying something you're—"

"Terrible at?" Po finished for him.

"No," Mantis started to deny it. "I was going to say . . ." Then he nodded. "That's actually what I was going to say."

"You really are good at cooking," Crane added.

"Well, I've been making noodles since I was three," Po told them. "I've been practicing kung fu for only a week. I've got the rest of my life to become just like you."

Po looked down, suddenly feeling embarrassed. He picked up his soup and took a giant gulp. When he lowered the bowl, Monkey let out a snicker.

"What?" Po demanded.

"Nothing, Master Shifu!" Mantis said.

The others burst out laughing. A noodle hung from Po's face, making it look as if he had long whiskers like Shifu.

Po laughed, too, and then started imitating the stern kung fu master. "Panda, you will never be the Dragon Warrior unless you lose five hundred pounds and brush your teeth!"

The Furious Five snickered, egging Po on.

"What is that noise you're making?" the panda went on, impersonating Shifu. "It's called laughter? I've never heard of it!"

Po reached over and grabbed two empty bowls. He held them up like ears. "Work hard, panda. And maybe, someday, you will have big ears like mine!"

Even Tigress couldn't stop herself from laughing a little.

Then, abruptly, the Furious Five all stopped laughing.

"What?" Po joked. "My ears are not working for you? I thought these ears were pretty good," he went on. "In fact . . ."

Monkey cleared his throat. "Po, it's Shifu," he whispered.

"Of course, it's Shifu!" Po replied. "Who else would I be imitating?"

A dead silence met his words.

With a sinking feeling, Po turned around slowly. To his dismay, Shifu stood there, fuming.

"Oooh! Master Shifu!" Po exclaimed. He slurped up the noodle mustache clinging to his lip.

Monkey couldn't help but let out a laugh.

"You think this is funny?" Shifu snarled.

"Tai Lung has escaped from prison, and you're here, acting like children!"

Po was stunned. "What?" he said. "Tai Lung escaped?"

"Yes!" Shifu answered. "He is coming for the Dragon Scroll, and you, panda, are the only one who can stop him."

Po started to laugh.

"Silly me!" he declared. "Here I am saying that you have no sense of humor, Shifu! I'm going to . . ."

Shifu stared back at Po, a deadly serious look on his face.

Slowly it sank in. Po swallowed hard. "You're not kidding, are you?" he said. "Tai Lung wants the Dragon Scroll, and I have to stop him?" He shook his head vigorously from side to side. "Master Oogway will stop him!" he added desperately. "He did it before; he'll do it again!"

"Oogway cannot stop him," Shifu replied. "Not anymore."

They all looked at Shifu, suddenly noticing that he was holding Oogway's staff.

"Oh no," Viper murmured. "Oogway is gone!"

"That's right," Shifu said. "And now our only hope is the . . . Dragon Warrior." He spat out the name.

"The panda?" Tigress said in a tone of disbelief.

"Yes, the panda!" Shifu answered.

Tigress looked pale. "Master, please," she started. "Let *us* stop Tai Lung. This is what you've trained us to do."

"No!" Shifu shook his head. "It is not your destiny to defeat Tai Lung, Tigress. It is *his*!"

He turned to point at Po, but the panda was gone.

"Where'd he go?" Shifu demanded, looking around the kitchen.

Po had run outside in record time. Despite everything Shifu and Oogway had told him about destiny, there was no way he could defeat a warrior like Tai Lung. The snow leopard would destroy him in seconds.

BLAM!

With an amazing kung fu leap, Shifu landed in front of Po.

"You cannot leave!" Shifu informed him. "A real warrior never quits!"

"Right!" Po retorted. He tried to maneuver around Shifu, but the kung fu master pushed him back.

"Come on!" Po said. "How am I supposed to beat Tai Lung? I can't even beat you to the stairs!"

"You will beat him because you are the Dragon Warrior!" Shifu declared.

"You don't believe that," Po said. "You never believed that. From the moment I got here, you've been trying to get rid of me."

"Yet you stayed," Shifu said, looking closely at Po. "You stayed because deep down inside you knew Oogway was right. You believed."

"No, I didn't!" Po shot back.

Shifu looked up, surprised.

"I stayed because every time you threw a brick at my head or said I smelled, it hurt," Po explained. "Especially the bricks!" he went on. "But it could never hurt more than it hurt every day of my life just being me."

Po looked down at the valley. "Down there I'm the fat, clumsy panda that everyone laughs at. I don't fit in my father's kitchen. I don't fit between the tables. I don't even fit in my pants!" He paused. "I used to imagine that, somehow, all these things were for a reason. That there was some destiny for me being so . . . *me*."

He stole a look at Shifu. "This has been the closest I've ever come to finding out. I guess I've learned that my fate is to be a fat, clumsy panda for the rest of my life."

"No!" Shifu declared. "I can train you. I will turn you into the Dragon Warrior."

"How?" Po demanded.

Shifu started to speak, and then stopped. "I don't know," he admitted.

"That's what I thought," Po said. "You can believe all you want, but you can't change me into something I'm not."

With that, the panda turned and walked away.

sixteen

Tigress paced outside the palace, watching Shifu. He stood in the moonlight under the peach tree, staring off into the darkness. He'd been there for hours, without moving.

Tigress could see that her master was deeply worried about Tai Lung's return. *I can help,* she thought, making up her mind about something.

She flew through the air, landing on a rooftop in the village below. Then she looked back at the palace.

"This is what you trained me to do, Shifu," she whispered. She took off, running.

Within minutes, the other four members of the Furious Five were right behind her.

"Tigress!" Viper called.

She kept going, and they chased after her.

"Don't try to stop me!" she yelled.

They raced through the village.

Crane shouted something at her.

"What?" she cried over her shoulder.

"We're not trying to stop you!" he called back.

"We're coming with you!" Viper added.

Tigress stopped to wait. "Thank you," she murmured when her friends finally caught up.

Then together they ran off into the night, ready for battle.

The next morning Shifu was sound asleep when loud noises woke him up. They were coming from inside the bunkhouse.

Shifu headed for the kitchen. As he rounded the corner, he could see Po's shadow doing kicks and spins.

"What in the world?" he murmured. It looked as if the panda were performing amazing kung fu stunts as he moved about the room.

When Shifu entered the kitchen, he saw Po stuffing his mouth with huge quantities of food.

Po stopped mid-munch. "What?" he asked with a shrug. "I eat when I'm upset, okay?"

Shifu watched the panda, an idea suddenly forming in his mind.

"Oh, no, panda," Shifu said eagerly. "There's no need to explain. I just thought you might be Monkey. He hides his almond cookies on the top shelf."

Then Shifu left the room, hiding just outside the doorway. He wanted to see if his hunch about the panda was correct.

KLUMP! KLONK! THUNK!

Shifu peeked back into the room—and

spotted Po perched on top of the high shelves. He was jamming almond cookies into his mouth as fast as he could.

Po looked over at Shifu with a guilty expression. "Don't tell Monkey, okay?" he said.

Shifu was grinning widely. "Look at you!" he exclaimed.

"I know," Po said sadly. "I disgust you."

"No, no, not at all," Shifu replied. "I just want to know, how did you get up there?"

Po shrugged. "I don't know. I—I just wanted a cookie, I guess," he said, popping another one into his mouth.

"And yet . . ." Shifu stepped closer, gazing at Po's position. The panda was sitting with his legs stretched out to each side. "You are ten feet off the ground, and you have done a perfect split."

"No." Po shook his head. "This was just an accident."

The two of them stared at each other for a second, each lost in his own thoughts. Then . . .

WHOMP! Po lost his footing and slammed to the floor.

Shifu thought of Master Oogway. "There are no accidents," he told Po. "Come with me, panda!"

Shifu led Po on a long trek up the mountain.

"I know you're trying to be all mystical and kung fuey," Po said, panting. "But could you at least tell me where we're going?"

Shifu didn't reply. He just kept walking, moving farther and farther ahead of Po.

When Po finally caught up, Shifu was waiting for him beneath a tree. Golden grass swayed in the wind, and nearby was a small pool of water.

Shifu breathed in the morning mist as Po approached.

"You dragged me all the way out here for a bath?" Po demanded. He dipped a paw into the pool and patted his armpits.

"Panda!" Shifu said sharply. "We do not wash our pits in the Pool of Sacred Tears."

"The Pool of Sacred Tears," Po echoed. He looked around, suddenly knowing just where he was.

"This is where Oogway unraveled the mysteries of harmony and focus," Shifu confirmed. "This is the birthplace of kung fu."

The two of them stood there for a moment, remembering the great master Oogway for a moment.

Then Shifu leaped onto a rock. "Do you want to learn kung fu?" he asked.

"Yes," Po answered.

"Then I am your master!" Shifu declared.

"Okay," Po said, tears of joy forming in his eyes. Finally, Shifu was taking him seriously.

"Don't cry," Shifu warned him.

Po sniffed. "All right," he said, nodding.

Shifu led him to an open field. "Now listen, panda," he said. "When you focus on kung fu, when you concentrate, you stink at it."

"Thanks a lot," Po said, scowling.

"But perhaps that is my fault," Shifu added

quickly. "I cannot train you the way I have trained the Furious Five. I now see the way to get through to you."

With that, he produced something from behind his back—a bowl of steaming hot soup.

Po's eyes lit up. "Oh, awesome! I'm so hungry!" he said.

Shifu laughed. "Good. When you have been trained, you may eat," he said. "Now let us begin."

SEVENTEEN

All day long, Shifu trained Po, taking him through all sorts of exercises— deep breathing, push-ups, sit-ups, climbing, and more, all while holding a bowl of food just out of Po's reach.

Finally, Shifu set a bowl of dumplings on a boulder. "After you, panda," Shifu said, gesturing toward the bowl.

Po stopped short, suspicious. "Just like that?" he asked the teacher. "I don't have to do any more sit-ups? Or take a ten-mile hike?"

"I vowed to train you," Shifu told him. "And you have been trained. You are free to eat."

Po grabbed one of the dumplings with his chopsticks. "Are you sure?"

"Enjoy," Shifu said, nodding.

Po raised the dumpling to his mouth, still hesitating just a little.

WHOOSH!

Just as he was about to eat it, Shifu snatched it away.

"Hey!" Po cried, as Shifu swallowed the dumpling.

"I said, you are free to eat," Shifu replied. "Have a dumpling."

Po reached for one—and Shifu leaped across the table and kicked it into the air.

"Hey!" Po said again.

Shifu ate it, making Po scowl again.

"You are free to eat!" Shifu declared.

Now Po was mad. "Am I?" he demanded.

"Are you?" Shifu challenged him.

Po and Shifu both grabbed their chopsticks.

Po slammed the table and sent the bowl of dumplings soaring into the air. As the dumplings rained down, Shifu leaped into the air and gobbled all of them, except for one.

Moving skillfully with newfound agility and speed, Po finally managed to get the last dumpling.

But instead of eating it himself, Po tossed the dumpling into Shifu's open hand.

"I'm not hungry . . . master," he said.

Shifu smiled. Then he and Po bowed respectfully to each other.

Tai Lung raced toward a rope bridge that stretched between two towering mountain peaks and over a body of water below. Halfway across, he paused. The Valley of Peace lay in the distance.

At last I have reached my destination, he thought triumphantly.

Just then, the Furious Five appeared on the other side of the bridge.

Tai Lung roared in fury. How dare they block his path!

"Cut the bridge!" Tigress called out.

The others slashed the ropes that held the bridge to the mountain. Tai Lung had almost made it across when Tigress sliced the final rope. Then she leaped toward the snow leopard, her claws extended.

The two cats tumbled toward the middle of the rope bridge as it began to fall into the canyon below.

The other four members of the Furious Five grabbed the support ropes and held on tightly.

Tai Lung growled at Tigress. "Where is the Dragon Warrior?"

Tigress stepped closer. "How do you know you're not looking at her?" she shot back.

Tai Lung laughed. "You think I'm a fool?" he said. "I know you're not the Dragon Warrior. None of you are!"

The Furious Five exchanged surprised looks. *Did Tai Lung know about the panda?* they wondered.

"That's right," Tai Lung went on confidently. "In my travels I heard about how he fell from the sky on a ball of fire. I also heard that he's a warrior unlike anything the world has ever seen."

This time the Furious Five exchanged confused looks.

"Po?" Monkey said tentatively. "Are you talking about Po?"

"So that's his name!" Tai Lung declared. "Finally, I'll face a worthy opponent. Our battle will be legendary!"

At that, Tigress charged. Tai Lung reacted quickly, fighting back with a spectacular block and then a series of powerful strikes and kicks.

Within minutes, a section of the bridge was wrapped around Tigress's neck.

"Go! Help Tigress!" Mantis told Viper and Crane. "Monkey and I can hold up the bridge."

Viper slithered toward Tai Lung, while Crane helped to free Tigress.

Wrapping herself around his arm, Viper used Tai Lung's own paw to punch the snow leopard again and again. "Let's see how you like it!" she said.

Tai Lung fought back. He caught Viper in a hold and circled his paws around her throat.

"Monkey!" Viper said in a choked voice. "Help me!"

Monkey was still helping Mantis hold up the rope bridge.

"Go," Mantis urged him. "I can manage."

Monkey leaped into action, swiftly kicking Tai Lung in the chest. Tigress came at Tai Lung again, but he sent her crashing through the slats of the bridge. In a flash Tai Lung was running toward them again on a single strand of rope.

"Mantis!" Tigress yelled.

Mantis reacted by whipping his end of the rope hard, sending a section of rope shooting toward Tai Lung. As the rope swirled around Tai Lung, the Five spotted their chance.

"Now!" Tigress shouted.

The Five all let out a loud roar. Then, all together, they went after Tai Lung, pounding him with fierce kicks and punches. Finally, Tigress slashed the rope between them. Tai Lung plummeted into the canyon below, dropping down . . . down . . . and then finally disappearing into the mist.

Mantis whipped his end of the rope, returning the others safely to the mountain.

The Furious Five looked at one another as they gasped for breath. They'd done it! They had stopped Tai Lung before he could enter the Valley of Peace!

Then Tigress's eyes suddenly went wide. The other end of the rope bridge was now rapidly circling the far mountain peak. That meant . . .

"Tai Lung!" she cried.

With a crash, the snow leopard stood before them again.

"Shifu taught you well," he said ominously. "But . . ." He jabbed a finger at Monkey, instantly paralyzing him. "He didn't teach you everything. . . ."

eighteen

That evening Shifu and Po walked through the palace courtyard. The panda was carrying a heavy backpack, but there was a happy spring in his step.

"You have done well, Po," Shifu complimented him.

"Done *well?*" Po repeated. "Are you kidding? I've done *awesome!*"

He swung his belly around and knocked Shifu off balance.

Shifu staggered backward, and then quickly

regained his dignity. "The mark of a true hero," he reminded Po solemnly, "is humility."

A second later, he leaned closer to Po and whispered in his ear, "But, yes, panda, you have done awesome!" Then he punched him playfully on the arm.

Together they laughed. Just then, a figure appeared in the sky over them.

It was Crane—and he was carrying the rest of the Five. A moment later, they all crashed to the ground.

"Guys!" Po cried out in alarm. He threw down his backpack and rushed over. "Are they dead?" As he bent over them, he could see that they were all still breathing and their eyes were open.

Crane struggled to lift his head. "We were no match for his nerve attack," he murmured, collapsing.

"He has gotten stronger," Shifu said gravely.

"Tai Lung?" Po asked. "Stronger?"

Shifu bent over Viper, working to release her

from the paralysis hold. Next were Mantis and Monkey.

"HE'S TOO STRONG!" Monkey yelled as he came to. He leaped to his feet and delivered a strong kung fu punch to Po's head.

Slowly, he looked around, realizing where he was. "He's too strong! And too fast!" he murmured.

Shifu kneeled over Tigress.

"I thought we could stop him," she said.

"He could have killed you all," Shifu said.

"Why didn't he?" Viper asked.

"So you could come back here and strike fear into our hearts," Shifu answered. "But it won't work!"

Po was still rubbing his sore head from where Monkey had hit him.

"Uh, it might work," he said. "A little, I mean. I'm pretty scared."

"You can defeat him, panda," Shifu retorted.

"Are you kidding?" Po shook his head. "If they can't stop him, how can I?" he said. "I mean, they're five *masters*, okay? I'm just one *me*."

"But you have one thing that no one else does," Shifu reminded him. "Come with me."

Confused, Po followed Shifu to the Scroll Room inside the Jade Palace. He looked up at the ceiling, where the carved dragon clutched the scroll in his mouth.

"Do you really believe that I'm ready?" Po asked Shifu, his own voice filled with doubt.

"You are ready, Po," Shifu answered firmly.

Their eyes locked, and Po nodded. Shifu and Oogway had told him it was his destiny. He must believe it, too.

nineteen

Shifu went over to get Oogway's staff, which hung in a rack surrounded by candles.

As Po and the Furious Five stood by, Shifu carried the staff over to the Water of the Moon pool. Shifu bowed his head. Then, with his eyes still closed, he raised the staff above his head.

An instant later, peach blossom petals rose from the pool in a flickering, whirling cloud. The gentle tornado spun toward the ceiling carving that held the Dragon Scroll. The petals swirled around, loosening the scroll from the dragon's mouth.

Before it hit the pool, Shifu reached out and caught it with the staff. Then he turned to Po, holding out the sacred document.

"Behold, the Dragon Scroll," he said solemnly. "It is yours."

"Wait," Po said nervously. "What happens when I read it?"

"No one knows for sure," explained Shifu, "but legend says you will become so powerful, you'll be able to hear a butterfly's wings beat."

"Really?" Po said eagerly. "That's cool!"

"Yes," Shifu replied. "And you will see light in the deepest cave. And feel the universe in motion around you."

"Wow! Can I punch through walls?" Po wanted to know. "Can I do a quadruple backflip? Will I have invisibility—"

"Focus," Shifu reminded him. "Focus."

"Okay . . ." Po looked away for a second, thinking about everything he'd learned today.

"Read it, Po, and fulfill your destiny," Shifu said to him. "Read it and become the Dragon Warrior!"

Po drew in a breath, suddenly nervous as he grasped the tube containing the scroll and tried to pull off the top.

It didn't budge. Po strained.

"It's impossible to open," Po said. He strained again. Then he tried to bite it off.

Watching him, Shifu sighed. Finally, he held out his hand and Po passed him the scroll. Without any effort, Shifu removed the top and passed the tube back to Po.

"Thank you," Po fumbled. "I probably loosened it up for you. Okay, here goes," he said, glancing at the Furious Five.

Monkey flashed him a thumbs-up.

As Po started to unroll the scroll, golden light bathed his face. Shifu stepped closer to him, waiting to see what would be revealed after all this time.

Po straightened out the scroll, and an

odd look crossed his face. And then, to the surprise of everyone in the room, he began to scream.

"AAAAAAAAAAGHHHH!"

They all looked at him in concern.

"What?" Shifu said. "What's wrong?"

"Here!" Po said, terrified. "Look at this!" He held up the scroll for Shifu to see.

"No!" Shifu immediately shielded his eyes and turned his head away. "I am forbidden to look upon the . . ."

But Shifu couldn't help himself. His eyes swung back to the scroll. Then he reached out and grabbed it from Po. He turned it upside down, and then closed it. As he opened it again, he made a startled sound.

"It's . . . it's *blank*," he burst out. "But Oogway said . . . He told me . . ." Shifu shook his head. "I—I don't understand."

The Furious Five stood there, still hurting and now devastated. Without unlimited power, there was no way that Po could stop a warrior like Tai Lung.

Po himself was nearly in tears. "So, Oogway was just a crazy old tortoise after all," he said.

Shifu's eyes were back on the scroll. "No," he said firmly. "Oogway was wiser than us all. There must be a message here that we are not seeing yet."

"Oh, come on, Shifu," Po said. "Face it, Oogway picked me by accident. Of course I'm not the Dragon Warrior. Who am I kidding?"

The Furious Five looked away, not knowing what to say or do.

"But who will stop Tai Lung?" asked Monkey.

"He'll destroy everything," Crane put in.

Shifu put the scroll back in its container and sealed it. He seemed strangely calm as he turned back to Po and gave him the scroll.

"Run," he commanded. "Run as fast as you can and as far as your legs will carry you."

Slowly, Po reached for the scroll.

"The rest of you," Shifu said, addressing the Furious Five, "evacuate the valley at once. You must protect the villagers from Tai Lung's rage."

"Master," Tigress said, concerned, "what about you?"

Shifu drew in a breath. "I will fight him."

"What?" Po shouted.

"I can hold him off long enough for everyone to escape," Shifu said.

"But, Shifu, he'll kill you," Po said.

"Then I will have finally paid for my mistake," Shifu replied.

Po and the Furious Five exchanged worried glances.

"Listen to me, all of you," Shifu continued. "It is time for you to continue your journey without me. I am very proud to have been your master."

Shifu saluted them and then turned away.

Po stood there, heartbroken.

Crane felt a wave of pity for him. He

stepped forward and put a wing around the panda, pulling him away.

Po resisted for a second. Then he let Crane and the others lead him out of the room.

twenty

The Furious Five immediately split up and began helping the villagers to evacuate.

Left on his own, Po made his way through the square. Crowds of villagers hurried past him with their things.

A few scowled at Po.

"Dragon Warrior, huh?" one said bitterly. "How come you aren't doing anything to save us?"

Po looked away, ashamed. He'd let everyone down, especially Oogway, Shifu, and the Furious Five.

"Hi, Dad," Po said when he reached the noodle shop.

Po's father looked up. "Po!" He ran over and wrapped his arms around his son.

Po bent down to hug him back.

"It's good to have you back, son!" his father said, wrapping an apron around Po's waist.

"It's good to be back," Po said flatly.

Po's father went back to packing up his noodle cart. Like everyone else, he was leaving the village as quickly as he could.

"Let's go, Po," he said. "I've been thinking—it's time to face facts. The future of noodles is dice-cut vegetables, not slices. At first, we'll be laughed at, but so has every pioneer."

Po's father started to walk off with the noodle cart. "Also, I was thinking that maybe this time we'll have a bigger kitchen," he went on, "one you can actually stand up in. Hmm? Wouldn't you like that?"

He turned and saw that Po hadn't moved. He walked back toward him.

"Son, I'm sorry things didn't work. It just wasn't meant to be."

Po's father took Po's hands in his. "Forget everything else," he said. "Your destiny still awaits. We are noodle folk—broth runs thick through our veins."

"I don't know, Dad," Po said with a sigh. "Honestly, sometimes I can't believe I'm actually your son."

His father looked stunned for a second. "Po, I think it's time I told you something that I should have revealed a long time ago."

Po looked at him and shrugged. "Okay."

His father paused dramatically. "It's the secret ingredient!" he blurted out. "Come here." He put his wing around Po. "The secret ingredient is . . ."

Po leaned closer to hear his father's closely guarded secret.

"Nothing!" his father blurted out.

"Huh?" Po stared at him.

"You heard me! Nothing!" His father repeated with a chuckle. "There is no secret ingredient!"

"Wait, wait!" Po couldn't believe it. "You mean, it's just plain old noodle soup? You don't add some kind of special sauce or anything else?"

"Nope," his father answered. "I don't have to. To make something special, son, you just have to *believe* it's special. It's all in the mind!" he went on, still grinning.

Po looked at his father, something dawning on him. Slowly, he picked up the Dragon Scroll and opened it.

Po stared down at the shiny parchment.

It's not really blank, he realized in a flash. Instead, filling the page was his own reflection.

"There is no secret ingredient," he said,

repeating his father's words out loud.

Then he glanced over at the window. In the distance, he could see the green roof tiles of the Jade Palace sitting up high above the village. At last, Po knew his destiny.

twenty-one

At dawn Shifu stood on the palace steps. He looked down upon the valley, awaiting his fate. And then, with a gust of wind, Tai Lung towered before him.

"I have come home, master," the snow leopard said in a mocking tone.

"This is no longer your home," Shifu informed him. "And I am no longer your master."

"Oh, that's right." Tai Lung sneered. "You have a new favorite. So where is this *Po*?" he asked, his voice dripping with disdain. "Did I scare him off?"

"This battle is between you and me," Shifu said firmly. "Leave Po out of it."

"So, that is how it's going to be," Tai Lung said.

"That is how it *must* be," Shifu answered.

At that, Tai Lung whirled around and pounced toward Shifu. They sparred for a few minutes, and then Tai Lung punched Shifu hard. He flew through the doors of the Jade Palace.

Shifu lay there on the hard floor, panting. Tai Lung circled around him.

"I rotted in jail for twenty years because of your weakness," the snow leopard said.

"Obeying your master is not weakness!" Shifu retorted.

"You knew I was the Dragon Warrior!" Tai Lung cried.

For a moment, they both flashed back to the past, remembering how a young Tai Lung had looked at Oogway expectantly, waiting to hear that he was indeed the Dragon Warrior. Instead, Oogway had surprised them both by shaking his head.

"When Oogway said otherwise," Tai Lung went on, "what did you do? What did you do?"

Tai Lung stared at Shifu, who turned away.

"NOTHING!" Tai Lung shouted the answer for him. "You did nothing!"

Shifu climbed to his feet, leaping into a kung fu stance. "You were not meant to be the Dragon Warrior!" he told Tai Lung. "That was not my fault!"

"NOT YOUR FAULT?!" Tai Lung bellowed. Enraged, he flung his arms around the room, knocking over dozens of kung fu artifacts and flinging them at Shifu.

"WHO FILLED MY HEAD WITH DREAMS?" Tai Lung yelled. "WHO DROVE ME TO TRAIN UNTIL MY BONES CRACKED? WHO DENIED ME MY DESTINY?"

Shifu managed to dodge each attack. "It was never my decision to make, Tai Lung!"

Tai Lung reached up and pulled Oogway's staff from the shrine. "It is now your decision to make!" he said ominously.

They sparred for several minutes until Tai Lung managed to pin Shifu down with the staff.

"Give me the scroll!" he bellowed.

"I would rather die," Shifu retorted.

The two grappled with the staff. Then, suddenly, it splintered into one hundred pieces.

As Shifu looked at the tiny splinters, he saw peach blossom petals flutter through the air. Caught off guard for a second, Shifu didn't see the strike coming from Tai Lung. Shifu was blasted into a column.

Dazed, Shifu somehow managed to scale the column, quickly reaching the ceiling. Tai Lung scrambled up right behind him, slamming into Shifu. Together they crashed through the roof, the tiny red panda grappling with the hulking snow leopard.

Outside, lightning shot through the sky as

Tai Lung and Shifu wrestled. Tai Lung wrapped his hands around Shifu's throat as they both sailed back through the roof.

They kicked apart. Shifu landed hard on the floor, while Tai Lung bounced off a wall and threw a lantern to the floor. Flames instantly whipped around the room.

Tai Lung's arms were ablaze as he charged at Shifu. "All I ever did, I did to make you proud!" he said between clenched teeth. "Tell me how proud you are, Shifu. Tell me! TELL ME!"

Before Shifu could reply, a fiery punch from Tai Lung sent him skidding across the floor.

BOOM!

He smashed into the reflecting pool.

Tai Lung stepped toward Shifu, his claws outstretched.

Shifu managed to lift his head. "I have always been proud of you, Tai Lung," he said weakly. "From the very first moment, I've been proud. In fact, it was my pride that blinded me. I loved you too much to see what you were becoming. I'm sorry."

Tai Lung stopped in his tracks.

Shifu waited, hoping that his words had somehow reached the snow leopard.

But Tai Lung's expression was still ice-cold as he stared at Shifu. "I don't want your apology!" he snarled. "I want my scroll!"

As he lifted Shifu toward the ceiling, his eyes suddenly narrowed in anger.

"The scroll is gone!" Tai Lung cried. "Where is the Dragon Scroll?"

He slammed Shifu to the floor.

"The Dragon Warrior has taken the scroll halfway across China by now," Shifu said, so weak by now he could barely get out the words. "You will never see that scroll, Tai Lung. Never."

"Aarrrgh!" Tai Lung howled in fury. He got down low, and then lunged at his former master.

Shifu closed his eyes, bracing himself for Tai Lung's violent attack.

Just then, a voice rang out. "Hey!"

Tai Lung and Shifu both looked up in surprise.

Standing in the doorway was Po. The giant panda huffed and puffed, trying to catch his breath as he clutched the Dragon Scroll in one hand.

"Whew!" he gasped. "I've got to get in shape. There are so many steps out there!"

twenty-two

Tai Lung cast Shifu aside and stared at Po. "Who are you?" he demanded.

"Buddy," Po said, still gasping for air. "I am the Dragon Warrior."

"You?" Tai Lung let out a low laugh and shot a look at Shifu. "He's a panda!" he exclaimed.

Tai Lung was still laughing as he turned back to Po. "You're a panda," he repeated. "What are you going to do, big guy? Sit on me?"

"Don't tempt me!" Po replied. "No, I'm going to use *this*," he said, holding up the Dragon Scroll.

Tai Lung's eyes went wide, and then he quickly made his move. Leaping across the room, he punched Po hard, knocking the scroll from his hands.

"Finally!" Tai Lung cried triumphantly.

Po bounced off a nearby pillar and slammed back into the snow leopard, sending him flying into a column.

Po struck a kung fu pose, setting himself for Tai Lung's next charge. But as the scary snow leopard came toward him, Po changed his mind, turning to run instead.

Tai Lung caught up with him outside the palace and made a grab for the scroll. Together they sailed off the steep steps in front.

Tai Lung delivered a powerful strike, sending Po flying onto the rooftop of a theater below.

Tai Lung dropped down in front of him. Po used the recoil move to whip back and smash

Tai Lung. The snow leopard skidded across the rooftop, but then came right back at Po.

"That scroll is mine!" he roared.

Tai Lung and Po bumped down the theater steps, chasing after the scroll.

Tai Lung leaped toward it, but Po grabbed some noodles from a street vendor and managed to snatch the scroll back using a noodle lasso.

Then Tai Lung knocked Po back through a grove of bamboo trees. As Po flew into a nearby wok shop, the scroll sailed out of his hands. Tai Lung started toward the scroll, but Po hid it, using some overturned woks like a shell game.

Tai Lung quickly hit away the woks and found the scroll. As the two of them grappled for it, Po slammed into a fireworks booth. Tai Lung lunged for the scroll. When he looked back to check on Po, he saw the panda flying through a fireworks-filled sky.

Po crashed into a rock wall—and Tai Lung. The scroll flew out of the snow leopard's hands and landed on a rooftop, right into the mouth of an ornamental dragon.

Po's training sessions with Shifu paid off now. Moving swiftly, Po scaled up the building in no time at all.

Tai Lung watched in amazement. "The scroll has given him power!" Tai Lung murmured. "He must be stopped!"

Tai Lung took a giant leap and punched the wall hard. A shock wave shuddered through the building, instantly collapsing it.

Po deftly skipped across falling roof tiles, reaching the scroll in midair.

But Tai Lung was fast, too. He raced after Po and unleashed a punishing blow. Po careened downward and hit the ground hard.

All around, buildings collapsed, burying them in a deep crater full of dust and debris.

When the dust settled, Po saw Tai Lung looming over him. "Finally!" the snow leopard cackled, clutching the scroll in one hand. "The scroll is mine!"

Po watched him unroll the famous scroll. Then he watched as Tai Lung's face fell.

"IT'S NOTHING!" the snow leopard bellowed. "The scroll says nothing!"

"You don't get it, do you?" Po said. He struggled to his feet. "There is no secret ingredient. There's no magic and no miracles. It's just me."

"*Rrraaaahhh!*" Tai Lung snarled and then lunged at Po. Po fought back, striking Tai Lung.

Desperately, Tai Lung attacked Po's nerve points, trying to paralyze him, but the panda's flab and thick fur got in the way.

Po just giggled. "Stop tickling me!" he cried.

At that, Tai Lung delivered a double-fisted punch to Po's belly.

The blow rippled through the panda. His arms swung back and then forward, striking Tai Lung, who crashed back into a building.

Po looked down at his hands, amazed by his own strength.

Tai Lung rose from the rubble and lunged

toward Po, but Po stopped him with the ultimate weapon—his huge iron belly!

The battered snow leopard snarled at Po. "You can't defeat *me*! You're just a big, fat panda!"

SHWING! Po grabbed Tai Lung's finger, and the snow leopard's eyes went wide with surprise.

"I'm not a big, fat panda," Po informed him. "I'm *the* big, fat panda!"

"The Wuxi Finger Hold!" Tai Lung declared.

"Oh, you know this hold?" asked Po.

"You're bluffing!" Tai Lung said. "Shifu never taught you the Wuxi Finger Hold!"

"You're right," Po said, shaking his head. "I figured it out on my own." He flexed his pinkie.

SKADOOSH!

twenty-three

A huge mushroom cloud had appeared over the Valley of Peace, cloaking it in mist. As news of Po's battle with Tai Lung spread, the villagers began to come out from hiding.

"Look!" someone cried. He pointed toward the mist, where a towering figure was emerging.

It was the warrior Po, wearing an upside-down wok for a hat and a torn apron for a scarf.

All around him villagers—and the Furious Five—began to cheer. The Dragon Warrior had triumphed! Peace had returned to the valley!

Po's father watched his son's approach with the rest of the villagers.

"That's my boy!" he declared proudly. "That big, fat, lovely panda is my son!"

He ran to Po, and the two of them hugged.

Just then, Po spotted the Furious Five among the crowd. "Hey, guys!" he said, waving.

Tigress bowed deeply. The other four followed her lead.

"Master," she murmured.

Po returned their bows. "Master," he echoed. Then he suddenly remembered something. "Master! Master Shifu!" he cried, racing toward the Jade Palace.

Po flew into the Scroll Room, out of breath again from his mad dash up the palace steps. Shifu lay on the floor there, his eyes closed.

"Master!" Po called. "Shifu! Shifu! Are you okay?"

Shifu stirred, and then slowly opened his eyes. "Po!" he said, smiling weakly. "You're alive! Either that or we're both dead."

"No, master," Po told him. "We're not dead. And guess what?" he added proudly. "I defeated Tai Lung!"

"You did?" Shifu shook his head, amazed. "It is just as Oogway foretold—you are the Dragon Warrior. You have brought peace to our valley. And to me. Thank you, Po."

Shifu's eyes fluttered closed. He lay there, still again.

"No!" Po cried in a panic. "No, no, no! Don't die, Shifu! Please!"

Shifu's eyes suddenly flew open. "I'm not dead, dummy—I mean, uh, Dragon Warrior," he said. "I'm simply being one with the universe. Finally."

"Oh," Po said. "So I, um, should stop talking?"

Shifu nodded. "Please. If you can."

"Okay," Po agreed, and Shifu closed his eyes again.

Po lay down companionably next to Shifu. For one full minute, Po actually managed to stay quiet.

But after that he couldn't stop himself.

"Want to get something to eat?" he blurted out.

With a sigh, Shifu opened his eyes. He looked at the giant panda affectionately and said, "Sure!"